Say Hola to Spanish at the Circus

written by
Susan Middleton Elya

illustrated by
Loretta Lopez

Lee & Low Books Inc. • New York

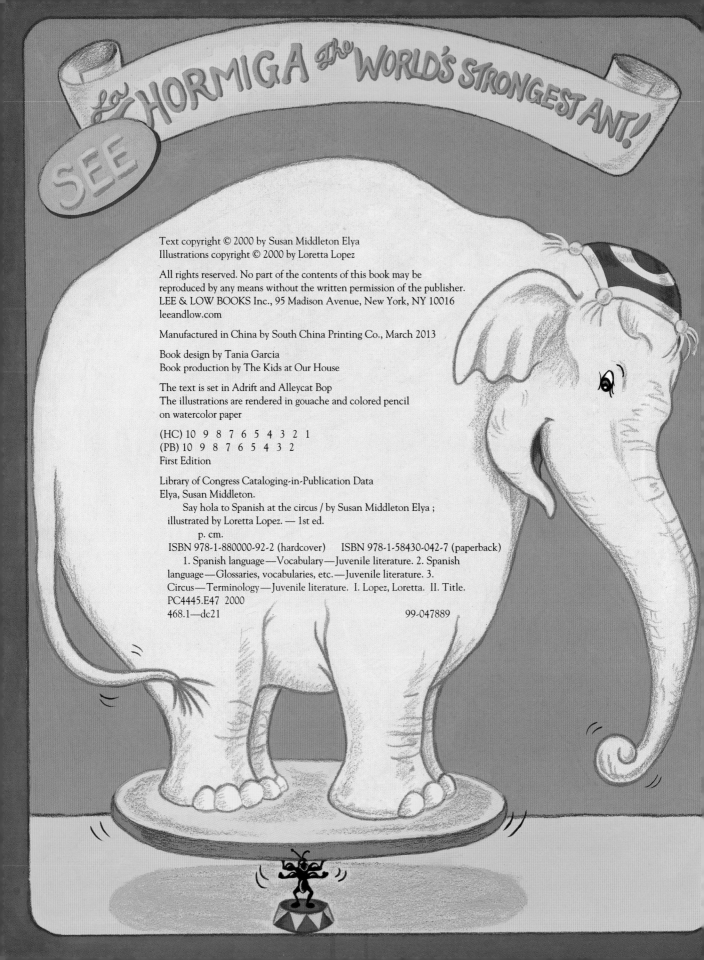

SEE La HORMIGA the WORLD'S STRONGEST ANT!

Manufactured in China by South China Printing Co., March 2013

Book design by Tania Garcia
Book production by The Kids at Our House

The text is set in Adrift and Alleycat Bop
The illustrations are rendered in gouache and colored pencil
on watercolor paper

(HC) 10 9 8 7 6 5 4 3 2 1
(PB) 10 9 8 7 6 5 4 3 2
First Edition

Library of Congress Cataloging-in-Publication Data
Elya, Susan Middleton.
    Say hola to Spanish at the circus / by Susan Middleton Elya ;
illustrated by Loretta Lopez. — 1st ed.
        p. cm.
    ISBN 978-1-880000-92-2 (hardcover)   ISBN 978-1-58430-042-7 (paperback)
        1. Spanish language—Vocabulary—Juvenile literature. 2. Spanish
language—Glossaries, vocabularies, etc.—Juvenile literature. 3.
Circus—Terminology—Juvenile literature. I. Lopez, Loretta. II. Title.
PC4445.E47 2000
468.1—dc21   99-047889

TWO HEADED SPACE ALIEN!

¡Hola!

¡Adiós!

Spanish is fun, so give it a try.
Hola is hello, adiós is good-bye.

Come to el circo. Bring tu mamá,
and tus hermanos, abuelos, papá.

Under the Big Top, laugh while payasos

wave with **sus pies** and walk with **sus brazos**.

You'll see spinning globos on noses of focas.

You'll watch the **leones** that open their **bocas**.

The tamer comes over, sticks in su cabeza.

Suppose the leones have una sorpresa!

The **música** plays, so lively and **fuerte.**

To wish him
good luck, you say,
"¡Buena suerte!"

¡Mira, qué grande! A big elefante!

He's dressed in gold tassles,

tan elegante.

Look! La jirafa has a long cuello.

How many humps
tiene el camello?

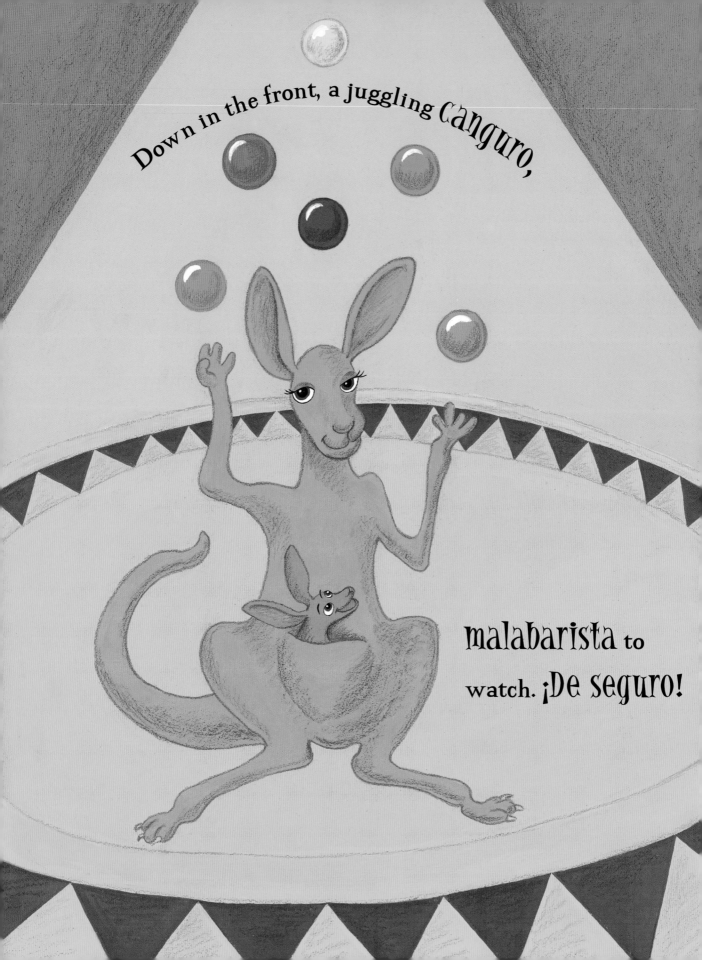

Down in the front, a juggling Canguro, malabarista to watch. ¡De seguro!

Feel like a snack?

¿Un perro caliente?

For your hot dog to last,

you chew lentamente.

A bag is a **bolsa**, a basket a **cesto**.

To ask, "What is this?"

you say, "**¿Qué es esto?**"

Behold chimpancés on their bicicletas.

Then look out for monos on motocicletas.

Up on the tightrope, un volatinero.

Down in one ring,
there's a monkey bombero.

Smoke is called humo.

Fire is fuego.

Douse them with agua.

¡Hasta luego!

Watch los trapecios above the whole place,

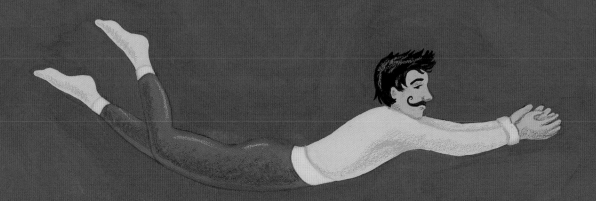

with three trapecistas—uno, dos, tres.

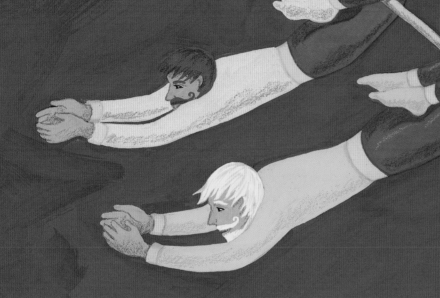

Piernas are legs and rodillas are knees.

They use them plus manos to grip the trapeze.

"¡Bravo!" you say. "¡Un acto tremendo!

¡Un circo fantástico, tan estupendo!"

After el circo,
the weather is bad.
Hace mal tiempo,
but you don't get mad.

¡Llueve! It's raining, big drops from the sky.

You've brought your paraguas to help you stay dry.

The raincloud is gray. La nube es gris.
Then out comes el sol and un arco iris.

Plants are called plantas.
A rose, una rosa.

There on the leaf — ¡Una mariposa!

Look at **el cielo**, the bright sky above you.

Tell someone special, **"Te quiero"** — I love you.

Hola is hello, adiós is good-bye.

Spanish is fun, so give it a try!

Glossary

abuelos (ah-BWEH-loce) grandparents

adiós (ah-dee-OCE) good-bye

agua (AH-gwah) water

bicicletas (bee-see-KLEH-tahs) bicycles

bocas (BOE-kahs) mouths

bolsa (BOLE-sah) bag

bombero (bome-BEH-roe) fireman

bravo (BRAH-voe) hurray

buena suerte (BWEH-nah SWEAR-teh) good luck

canguro (kahn-GOO-roe) kangaroo

cesto (SEHS-toe) basket

chimpancés (cheem-pahn-SEHS) chimpanzees

cuello (KWEH-yoe) neck

de seguro (DEH seh-GOO-roe) for sure

dos (DOSE) two

el cielo (EHL see-EH-loe) the sky

el circo (EHL SEER-koe) the circus

el sapo (EHL SAH-poe) the toad

el sol (EHL SOLE) the sun

elefante (ehl-eh-FAHN-teh) elephant

focas (FOE-kahs) seals

fuego (FWEH-goe) fire

fuerte (FWEHR-teh) strong, loud

globos (GLOE-boce) spheres, balloons

hace mal tiempo (AH-seh MAHL tee-EHM-poe) the weather is bad

hasta luego (AHS-tah loo-WEH-goe) good-bye, until later

hola (OE-lah) hello

humo (OO-moe) smoke

la hormiga (LAH ohr-MEE-gah) the ant

la jirafa (LAH hee-RAH-fah) the giraffe

la nube es gris (LAH NOO-beh EHS GREECE) the cloud is gray

lentamente (lehn-tah-MEHN-teh) slowly

leones (leh-OE-nehs) lions

llueve (yoo-WEH-veh) it's raining

los trapecios (LOCE trah-PEH-see-oce) the trapezes

malabarista (mah-lah-bah-REE-stah) juggler

manos (MAH-noce) hands

mira qué grande (MEE-rah KEH GRAHN-deh) look how big

monos (MOE-noce) monkeys

motocicletas (moe-toe-see-KLEH-tahs) motorcycles

música (MOO-see-kah) music

papá (pah-PAH) dad

paraguas (pah-RAH-gwahs) umbrella

payasos (pah-YAH-soce) clowns

piernas (pee-EHR-nahs) legs

plantas (PLAHN-tahs) plants

qué es esto (KEH EHS EHS-toe) what is this

rodillas (rroe-DEE-yahs) knees

su cabeza (SOO kah-BEH-sah) his head

sus brazos (SOOCE BRAH-soce) their arms

sus pies (SOOCE pee-EHS) their feet

tan elegante (TAHN ehl-eh-GAHN-teh) so elegant

tan estupendo (TAHN ehs-too-PEHN-doe) so stupendous

te quiero (TEH kee-EH-roe) I love you

tiene el camello (tee-EH-neh EHL kah-MEH-yoe) does the camel have

tío (TEE-oe) uncle

trapecistas (trah-peh-SEE-stahs) trapeze artists

tres (TREHS) three

tu mamá (TOO mah-MAH) your mom

tus hermanos (TOOCE ehr-MAH-noce) your brothers and sisters

un acto tremendo (OON AHK-toe treh-MEHN-doe) a tremendous act

un arco iris (OON AHR-koe EER-eece) a rainbow

un circo fantástico (OON SEER-koe fahn-TAHS-tee-koe) a fantastic circus

un perro caliente (OON PEH-rroe kah-lee-EHN-teh) a hot dog

un volatinero (OON voe-lah-tee-NEH-roe) a tight-rope walker

una mariposa (OO-nah mah-ree-POE-sah) a butterfly

una rosa (OO-nah RROE-sah) a rose

una sorpresa (OO-nah sohr-PREH-sah) a surprise

uno (OO-noe) one